Littlest Pet Shop™

LIFE'S Littlest LESSONS

by Ellie O'Ryan
illustrated by Jim Talbot

SCHOLASTIC INC.

New York   Toronto   London   Auckland   Sydney
Mexico City   New Delhi   Hong Kong   Buenos Aires

[handwritten inscription:] Happy Birthday! Dear Ruby — Page 18 "Memory Box" is a good idea for you to make to keep a sample of each of your cards and paintings! love Aunt Jasson

ISBN-13: 978-0-439-89753-2
ISBN-10: 0-439-89753-X

Littlest Pet Shop © 2007 Hasbro.
LITTLEST PET SHOP and all related characters
and elements are trademarks of and © Hasbro.
All Rights Reserved.

Published by Scholastic Inc. SCHOLASTIC and associated logos
are trademarks and/or registered trademarks of Scholastic Inc.

12 11 10 9 8 7 6 5 4 3 2 1   7 8 9 10 11/0

Interior book design by Two Red Shoes Design

Printed in Singapore
First printing, March 2007

Contents

"HITCH YOUR WAGON TO A STAR!"

— Ralph Waldo Emerson (1803–1882),
American author, poet, and philosopher

It's Your Life!

Sometimes it's happy.
Sometimes it's sad.
But it's always about you!
Everything that happens in your life,
from the good to the bad, is a lesson you
can learn for the future. So grab your
favorite pets and get ready for some
fun and inspiration as you
learn a little more
about yourself!

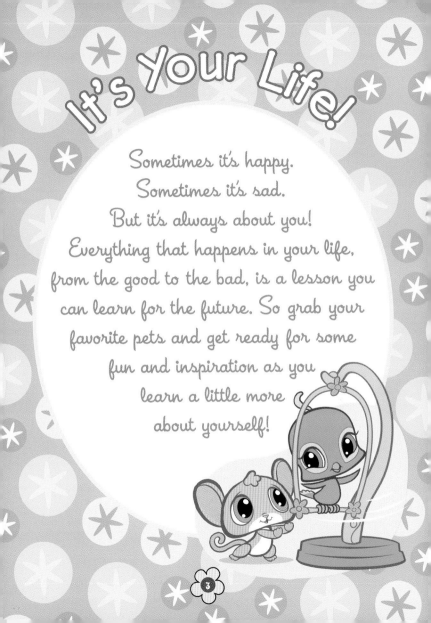

WHAT MAKES YOU AND YOUR LIFE Unique?

Grab a pen and a piece of paper and answer the questions below!

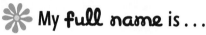 My **full name** is . . .

My **birthday** is . . .

 My **favorite pet** is . . .

 My **favorite color** is . . .

 My **favorite food** is . . .

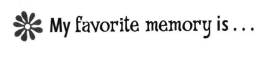 My favorite memory is . . .

 My favorite hobby is . . .

 My favorite sport is . . .

※ My favorite outfit is . . .

※ My favorite
person is . . .

A GIRL'S BEST FRIEND

Everyone knows that a pet can be the *best friend you'll ever have!* In fact, a pet will be such an IMPORTANT part of your life that you'll want to make sure the pet you pick will fit your personality. To find out which pet is your **BEST MATCH**, take this quiz.

1. These words best describe me:
   a) Playful and active.
   b) Quiet and shy.
   c) Cuddly and friendly.
   d) Free-spirited and exciting.

2. I like to spend a Saturday afternoon:
   a) At the park, the beach, or the mountains.
   b) Curled up with a good book.
   c) Sharing laughs with a best friend.
   d) Trying something new and exciting!

3. My dream vacation would include:
   - a) **Camping under the stars.**
   - b) **A visit to a spa.**
   - c) **An amusement park.**
   - d) **A tropical island.**

4. My clothing style is:
   - a) **Sporty and fun.**
   - b) **Designer chic.**
   - c) **Anything comfortable.**
   - d) **Adventurous and exotic.**

5. Some of my favorite colors are:
   - a) **Blue and red.**
   - b) **Pink and purple.**
   - c) **Orange and yellow.**
   - d) **Green and crimson.**

6. When I grow up, my dream job would be:
   - a) **Athlete.**
   - b) **Movie star.**
   - c) **Comedian.**
   - d) **Explorer.**
   - e) Artist
   - f) Clothes Designer

ALL DONE?

Now add up the number of A's, B's, C's, and D's. Then read on to find out which pet is *perfect* for you!

Answer Key:

IF you picked **mostly A's**, a playful puppy is the perfect pet for your active, fun life!

If you picked **mostly B's**, go for a sweet little kitty that will love quiet time and pampering – just like you do.

If you picked **mostly C's,** a funny hamster will keep you — and everyone you know — laughing.

If you picked **mostly D's,** an exotic bird will perfectly match your free-spirited style.

WHAT'S YOUR *Sign?*

Your birthday is just one thing that makes your life **unique**. Some people believe that the day on which you were born can actually influence your personality! Check out your **astrological sign** to see if the predictions are true.

AQUARIUS
(January 21–February 19)
Aquarius is accepting, joyful, and unpredictable. Aquarius people tend to get along well with Littlest Pet Shop frogs.

PISCES
(February 20–March 20)
Pisces is mysterious, spiritual, and empathetic. Pisces people tend to get along well with Littlest Pet Shop fish.

ARIES
(March 21–April 20)
Aries is impulsive, original, and pioneering. Aries people tend to get along well with Littlest Pet Shop monkeys.

TAURUS
(April 21–May 20)
Taurus is caring, thoughtful, and unique. Taurus people tend to get along well with Littlest Pet Shop dogs.

GEMINI
(May 21–June 21)
Gemini is smart, lively, and outspoken. Gemini people tend to get along well with Littlest Pet Shop birds.

CANCER
(June 22–July 22)
Cancer is sensitive, dreamy, and emotional. Cancer people tend to get along well with Littlest Pet Shop hermit crabs.

LEO
(July 23–August 22)
Leo is creative, confident, and ambitious. Leo people tend to get along well with Littlest Pet Shop cats.

VIRGO
(August 23–September 22)
Virgo is careful, witty, and a problem-solver. Virgo people tend to get along well with Littlest Pet Shop ferrets.

LIBRA
(September 23–October 22)
Libra is fair, charming, and generous. Libra people tend to get along well with Littlest Pet Shop rabbits.

SCORPIO

(October 23–November 22)
Scorpio is intense, powerful, and serious. Scorpio people tend to get along well with Littlest Pet Shop iguanas.

SAGITTARIUS

(November 23–December 21)
Sagittarius is optimistic, wise, and honest. Sagittarius people tend to get along well with Littlest Pet Shop turtles.

CAPRICORN

(December 22–January 20)
Capricorn is ambitious, driven, and responsible. Capricorn people tend to get along well with Littlest Pet Shop hamsters.

"The mere sense of living is joy enough."

— Emily Dickinson (1830–1886),
American poet

Memory-Maker

They say an elephant never forgets, and neither should you! While you're busy living, memories are being made – so take a minute or two to make sure they'll last a lifetime by taking a photo, keeping a journal, or creating a memory box.

WRITE AND *Remember*

Don't let those memories slip away! Writing in *a journal* is a great way to keep track of the things that happen in your life.

✳ A diary with **a lock** is a good choice if you have brothers, sisters, or a curious pet!

✳ Having trouble thinking of what to write? **Try using a calendar,** and just write a few notes every day.

Thursday	Friday	Saturday
1 Wore my favorite blue shirt today. Got an A- on a quiz!	**2** Pizza for lunch! Took my puppy for a walk after school.	**3** Went to the movies with my best friends—FUN!
8	**9**	**10**

※ Feeling artistic? Fill your journal with doodles and drawings!

✻ Gotta get it down *NOW?* Any old notebook will work. Just grab a pen and write!

MEMORY BOX

From ticket stubs to top secret notes to newspaper clippings, you'll want to save all the *special mementos* of your life. A memory box is the perfect place to keep them safe! Make sure you get an adult's permission before starting this craft.

You will need:

* Shoe box
* Wrapping paper and/or magazine cutouts
* Tissue paper
* Tape or glue
* Ruler
* Pencil
* Scissors
* Stickers

1. Measure each side of the shoe box's interior with the ruler.

2. Cut out pieces of tissue paper to fit each interior side of the shoe box and the shoe box lid. Glue or tape them into place.

3. Wrap the outside of the shoe box and the outside of the shoe box lid with wrapping paper, or cover it in artwork clipped from magazines.

4. For extra fun, add some stickers!

5. Once the glue is dry, put all of your mementos inside to keep them safe.

"Memory is the treasury and guardian of all things."

— Marcus Tullius Cicero (106–43 BC),
Roman orator, statesman, and poet

Dream a Little Dream

Nobody knows
what the future holds,
but that doesn't mean you can't
have fun dreaming about it!

Dream Signs
AND SYMBOLS

Some people believe that the dreams you have while you're asleep are full of *information*. If you see one of these pets in one of your dreams, here's what it means:

Bird
You have a sunny, happy outlook on life.

Cat
You really like someone.

Dog
You're about to make a great new friend.

Crab
You are persistent and you go after what you want.

Frog
Something unexpected is about to happen.

Fish
You're about to have good luck.

Rabbit
Something nice is going to happen.

AND HERE ARE A FEW MORE COMMON DREAM SIGNS AND SYMBOLS AND WHAT THEY MEAN!

Birthday
A surprise is coming your way!

Flying
You've risen above something or gained a different perspective on things.

School
There is something you need to learn.

Music
There is happiness in your life.

REACH FOR THE
stars!

GOT GOALS? Of course you do! It's never too early to start focusing on your future. You can start paving the way to your loftiest goals right now!

🌸 **First figure out what your goal is.** You may know exactly what you want in life, or your future may still seem a little hazy. Either way is okay — just keep thinking and dreaming until the path you want to take becomes clear.

🌸 Once you've identified your goal, **write down a list of things** you can do to make it come true.

🌸 **Keep your eyes on the prize!** Don't let that to-do list collect dust. If your dream is worth achieving, it's worth working to make it happen.

❀ **Never lose hope!** Some dreams take months or even years to achieve. If you keep believing, you can make just about anything a reality!

Go confidently in the direction of your dreams. Live the life you've imagined.

— Henry David Thoreau (1817–1862),
American author

Bright Little Star!

Everyone's got a creative spark inside— it's time to find yours and help it grow into a bright, shining star!

PET APARTMENT!

Put your creativity to good use by making your pets a **deluxe hangout.** You can even use items you have around the house! Make sure you get an adult's permission before you start this craft.

You will need at least some of the following:

- 🌸 **A shoe box**
- 🌸 Wrapping paper
- 🌸 Scissors
- 🌸 **Glue or tape**
- 🌸 **An old T-shirt or towel that can be cut up (make sure you get an adult's permission first!)**
- 🌸 **Assorted small boxes**
- 🌸 Cotton balls
- 🌸 Ribbon
- 🌸 **Tissue paper**
- 🌸 Old magazines

1. "Wallpaper" your pet's apartment by gluing or taping the wrapping paper to the inside of the box.

2. Cover the "floor" with wrapping paper, or cut scraps from the T-shirt or towel for throw rugs.

3. Make **tables and** other **furniture** using the assorted smaller boxes. Make a bed by filling a box with cotton and adding tissue-paper sheets and a blanket made out of a thick piece of ribbon.

4. Clip photos from magazines and hang them on the walls as **portraits.**

5. Welcome your pets into their brand-new home!

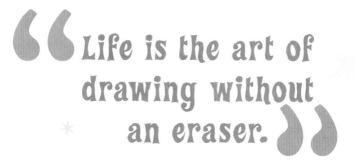

"Life is the art of drawing without an eraser."

— John W. Gardner (1912–2002), former American Secretary of Health, Education, and Welfare

Work Hard, Play Hard!

School, friends, family, hobbies, sports— *PHEW!* That's a lot to fit into one life. It's all about balance, so don't forget to play as hard as you work!

FIND THE TIME

If you feel like you've got too much going on, check out this list for some suggestions on *time management*. Now you can do even more in less time — perfect!

❇ Make a list of things you **NEED** to do and things you **WANT** to do. Tackle the "need" list first, then have fun doing the things on the "want" list.

❇ Figure out how long your list will take, then use a **calendar** to schedule your day. (Don't forget to include breaks!)

❇ Set specific goals to stay on track for accomplishing the things you really want to do.

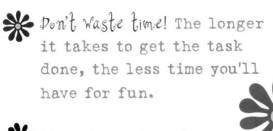

❋ Don't waste time! The longer it takes to get the task done, the less time you'll have for fun.

❋ if you hit a stumbling block, **take a break** or try doing a different task.

TAKE A BREAK!

Got downtime but don't know what to do with it? Grab a piece of paper and a pencil and **take this quiz** to find out!

1. You have a day off from school! How do you want to spend it?
    a. Sleeping late and watching TV.
    b. Shopping or hanging out with friends.
    c. Outdoors on a hiking adventure.

2. Yay! You finished your homework early! What do you want to do now?
    a. Catch a catnap—all that studying was *exhausting*!
    b. Call a friend or chat online.
    c. Take a walk or run around the block.

3. Recess is the time for:
    a. Resting your brain.
    b. Catching up with friends.
    c. Burning off all that pent-up energy.

34

4. If you were stranded on a tropical island with your friends, you'd want to:

    a. Stretch out in the sun and catch some rays.
    b. Plan a beach party.
    c. Lead an expedition to explore the island.

Answer Key:

If you picked **mostly A's,** you're in serious need of some rest and relaxation. Don't push yourself so hard that you forget to refuel!

If you picked **mostly B's,** it's high time you caught up with your pals. Remember that social time is important, too!

If you picked **mostly C's,** spend your downtime in action by getting outside and moving around!

WHAT PETS Need

All pets need food, fresh water, a cozy shelter—and lots of love, of course! But do you know what else pets would like to have? See if you can match up these pets and their favorite things!

1. Leash, ball, bone

2. Pink satin pillow, sparkly collar, mouse toy

3. Chew sticks, running wheel, wood chips

4. Perch, mirror, swing

A

B

C

D

"Think you can,
think you can't;
EITHER WAY
you'll be
RIGHT."

—Henry Ford (1863–1947),
American businessman and innovator

38

Happy Days and Tough Stuff

Life is made up of
good days and bad days.
Hopefully you'll have more of the good
ones, but it never hurts to know
how to handle the bad ones
when they pop up.

FEELING Sad?

It happens to everyone from time to time. No matter what's got you down, try to remember that this, too, will pass. And in the meantime, here's a list of tips and tricks to help you feel better ASAP.

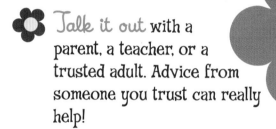

Talk it out with a parent, a teacher, or a trusted adult. Advice from someone you trust can really help!

Call a friend and *make plans.* You'll be having fun before you know it.

Clear your mind by writing down your **FEELINGS** in a journal.

 Do something—ANYTHING!—that you really love, from reading a good book to watching a favorite movie to painting your nails. Getting your mind off your worries can help you feel better.

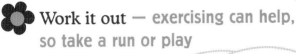 Work it out — exercising can help, so take a run or play a game!

Laugh IT UP!

Need a laugh? Try out these **funny jokes** about your favorite pets — then try making up your own!

🌸 How do turtles talk to each other?
THEY USE SHELL PHONES!

🌸 What is a cat's favorite dessert?
MICE CREAM!

🌸 What do you call a dog that plays in the snow?
A PUP-SICLE!

How did the fish buy a birthday present for his friend? **WITH A SAND DOLLAR!**

What kind of music do rabbits like best? **HIP-HOP!**

What did the frog want with his hamburger? A SIDE ORDER OF FRENCH FLIES!

IT'S A COLORFUL LIFE

Did you know that colors have meanings? **Whatever you're feeling, there's a color to match it.** In fact, you can even change your mood by surrounding yourself with a different color. Check out the list below when you need a little help deciding which color matches your mood!

RED is the color of passion, intensity, and excitement. People think of power and determination when they see the color red.

PINK stands for sweetness and happiness, as well as friendship and romance!

ORANGE is full of energy and enthusiasm.

YELLOW brings joy and happiness. Add some cheer to your day with a strand of sunny yellow beads or a bright yellow T-shirt!

GREEN is a restful color that symbolizes nature and growth. It can also mean hope and life.

BLUE brings calm and relaxation. This color also symbolizes trust, loyalty, and intelligence.

PURPLE is the color of wisdom, creativity, and originality. As the official color of royalty for hundreds of years, purple is also the color of luxury and ambition.

"Every day is a good day."

—Yunmen Wenyan (862 or 864–949), Chinese Buddhist monk and Zen master

Make It Count!

Every day is a chance to live your life to the fullest. Don't let anything stand in your way! After all, it's your life – no one can live it better than YOU!